HORRIBLE HARRY
and the Missing Diamond

Other Books by Suzy Kline

HORRIBLE HARRY
and the Missing Diamond

BY SUZY KLINE
PICTURES BY AMY WUMMER

VIKING
An Imprint of Penguin Group (USA) Inc.

VIKING

An imprint of Penguin Young Readers Group
Published by the Penguin Group
Penguin Group (USA) Inc.
375 Hudson Street
New York, New York 10014, U.S.A.

USA / Canada / UK / Ireland / Australia / New Zealand / India / South Africa / China
Penguin Books Ltd, Registered Offices: 80 Strand, London WC2R 0RL, England

For more information about the Penguin Group visit www.penguin.com

First published in the United States of America by Viking,
an imprint of Penguin Young Readers Group, 2013

LIBRARY OF CONGRESS CATALOGING-IN-PUBLICATION DATA
Kline, Suzy.
Horrible Harry and the missing diamond / by Suzy Kline ; illustrated by Amy Wummer.
p. cm.
Summary: "Best friends Harry and Doug must find their teacher's missing diamond in
time for the class talent show."—Provided by publisher.
ISBN 978-0-670-01426-2 (hardcover)
[1. Lost and found possessions—Fiction. 2. Talent shows—Fiction. 3. Schools—Fiction.
4. Ability—Fiction.] I. Wummer, Amy, ill. II. Title.
PZ7.K6797Hnqm 2013 [E]—dc23 2012031078

Manufactured in China

1 3 5 7 9 10 8 6 4 2

Set in New Century Schoolbook LT Std

The publisher does not have any control over and does not assume any responsibility
for author or third-party websites or their content.

Dedicated to
my very loving and handsome grandson
Holden David Hurtuk.
Thank you for all the joy
you bring to my daily life.
I love you!
Gamma

Special appreciation and thanks . . .

To Old Farmers Road School in Long Valley, New Jersey, where I got the missing diamond seed for this story.

To Mrs. Lombo and my granddaughter Gabby's fourth grade class at Peter Woodbury Elementary School in Bedford, New Hampshire, for giving me the teacher's chocolate drawer idea!

To my granddaughter Saylor, who had a great third grade "talent show" birthday party.

To Jamie at Wheelock School in Medfield, Massachusetts, who suggested the title "Horrible Harry and the Quadruple Revenge" for Doug's next story.

To my patient and caring husband, Rufus, who talked to me many times about my writing.

And to my very hardworking editor, Leila Sales, who helped me greatly.

A heartfelt thank you!

Contents

What's Your Talent?

When something is missing, I usually know where to look for it.

Like a sock.

Mom's keys.

Or a library book.

But what if the thing you're missing is your talent? Where do you look for that?

My name is Doug, and I write stories about my best friend, Harry, and me in

Room 3B. This story is about two missing things that were very valuable and
very hard to find.

The ending was a big surprise to me.
I couldn't believe *where* we found them.

It all started with a sign that was
posted on our classroom bulletin board
two weeks ago:

WHAT'S YOUR TALENT?
Share it with our two third grade classes
on April 10th

Miss Mackle said that everyone had
to do something, and that we would
host the show in our room. I didn't have
a clue what I could do.

Play the piano? No, I'd only had two
lessons.

Share my artwork? The only things I can draw well are tepees.

Do a magic trick? I couldn't pull a rabbit out of a hat, or a quarter from behind my ear.

Sing or dance? No way! I'd rather be backstage.

Now it was two days before the talent show, and I still didn't know what my act would be. It was silent reading time and Dexter's turn to sit in the blue beanbag chair. He looked very comfortable, sprawled out with his biography of

Elvis Presley. Maybe Dexter would sing an Elvis song for his talent.

Harry was reading a Hardy Boys book, *Mystery of Smugglers Cove.* Harry loves being a detective. He could demonstrate how a private eye cracks a case for his talent. Or he could do an animal show with his creepy pets: a tarantula, a milk  snake, and a giant African millipede. Harry knows lots of fascinating facts about those horrible critters.

Mary was reading *The Guidebook of Fabulous Hairdos.* She could style someone's hair for the talent show. On St. Patrick's Day, she had given Harry a green spiked hairdo.

I looked at the teacher, Miss Mackle. She was reading a big picture book at her desk in the back of the room. She always did that the first ten minutes of silent reading. When she finished looking at the picture book, she left her desk, then went up to her big chair in front of the class and began reading a chapter book.

I couldn't think about the talent show anymore. It was time to give my brain a break. I opened my book, *The Indian in the Cupboard*, and began reading where I left off.

It was so peaceful for the next three minutes.

Then Song Lee shrieked!

The Lost Diamond

Song Lee's scream startled everyone. Sidney and Ida dropped their books.

"Miss Mackle!" Song Lee blurted out. She was pointing to Miss Mackle's left hand.

The teacher glanced down at her engagement ring. It had three diamonds. Only when she looked at it now, she froze.

"My middle diamond is missing!" she exclaimed.

Everyone gasped.

Harry popped out of his seat and immediately started questioning the teacher like Sergeant Friday on old-time TV. Harry really did have a talent for being a nosy detective.

"When did you last see all three diamonds?" he asked.

The teacher seemed stunned. She didn't even tell Harry to sit down. "Why . . . just this morning, in the Teachers' Room. I was showing my engagement ring to the new art teacher, Mrs. Matalata. I was telling her how it belonged to my fiancé's grandmother." The teacher sighed. "All three diamonds were there, *then*."

"Did you leave the building at lunchtime?" Harry inquired.

"No."

"Did you go outside to the playground?"

"No. I've been indoors all day."

"*So . . .*" Harry raised a finger. "You lost it here *at South School, today.*" He took out a notebook and jotted something down.

Miss Mackle shook her head as she stared at her ring.

Harry continued his questioning.

"Retrace your steps. Where have you been the past four and a half hours?"

Man, I thought, *if I could be an investigator like Harry, I could find my talent!*

Miss Mackle closed her book. "That's pretty easy, actually. The Teachers' Room, the hallway, and . . . Room 3B."

Harry wasn't satisfied. "No other place? You're sure?"

"Well, the teachers' bathroom."

Lots of kids giggled but not Harry. He was all business. He added another fact to his pocket notebook. "Okay!" he concluded. "Can we start here in Room 3B?" he asked.

Miss Mackle looked at the rest of us. "Boys and girls, do you want to help look for my diamond?"

"*Yes!*" we shouted.

"I'll set my timer for eight minutes," the teacher announced. "I don't want to take up too much class time."

Sid leaped out of his seat, throwing one fist high in the air. "The search begins!"

The Search Begins

I grabbed my journal and started listing places where kids searched. I wanted to save the details for a future story.

Harry made a beeline for the garbage can.

Song Lee and ZuZu dropped to their knees and began hunting for the teacher's diamond on the floor. Mary examined the moon rug in the library corner.

Dexter scanned the beanbag chair. Ida danced around the room, twirling and pointing her toes. I don't think she was looking for anything. I think Ida was just practicing her talent show act.

Suddenly Sidney yelled, "I found it!"

Everyone stopped and looked at him. He was by the sink.

"Oops, sorry," he said. "It's just a silver star sticker."

Miss Mackle put a hand over her heart.

Harry got out pieces of newspaper from the art supply bin and dumped the garbage can onto them.

"Harry!" Mary objected, "You're making a mess!"

"No, that's a good idea," Miss Mackle said, and she joined him. Together they went through every scrap of paper, every

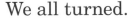

pencil stub, broken crayon, wrapper, and plastic snack bag.

"I found it!" Sidney called out again.

We all turned.

"Ohhh," he groaned, "it's just some glitter."

Mary marched up to him. "Sidney LaFleur," she said firmly, "will you puhleese double-check before you call out again. You're giving me a heart attack!"

Harry took out his magnifying glass from under his T-shirt. The magnifying glass hung from an old army dogtag chain around Harry's neck. His great-grandpa Spooger wore that chain in World War II. Harry studied each crumpled-up piece of masking tape that stuck to the sides of the garbage can. "Did you tape something to the bulletin board this morning before the bell?"

"Yes, new name cards for the monitor chart," Miss Mackle answered.

"Did you mess up some of the tape?" Harry quizzed.

"I did."

"Well," Harry replied, "one of these sticky globs could be hiding your diamond! I'm sure they loosened it."

Miss Mackle must have agreed, because she sat down on the floor and began looking closely at the masking tape, too.

A few minutes later, she got up and went to her desk. She wrote something on a pink piece of paper, then held it up.

"Does anyone know where Mr. Beausoleil's mailbox is?" she asked.

Harry was the only one who answered. "It's right outside the boiler room," he announced. "On the left side of his door."

"Yes!" Miss Mackle replied. She handed the note to Harry. "Please take this down to him. If he's not there, just leave it in his box. I want the custodian to know about my missing diamond."

Harry bolted out the door just as the oven timer buzzed on the teacher's desk.

"Boys and girls," Miss Mackle called

out. "Thank you for trying to look for my diamond. Unfortunately, things get lost. We just have to carry on."

So we all went back to our silent reading. I don't think the teacher read much, though. She only turned the page once.

When Harry didn't return shortly, I started to get worried. Was Harry snooping somewhere he shouldn't?

I held up one finger. That meant I was asking permission to go to the bathroom. As soon as Miss Mackle noticed my hand sign, she nodded a yes.

Then I took off. I had to find Harry before he got into trouble!

Where's Harry?

As soon as I got to the boiler room, I could see the pink note sticking out of Mr. Beausoleil's mailbox. Harry had been there already. I checked the boys' bathroom but Harry wasn't there.

I raced up the stairs to the main hallway. When I got to the Teachers' Room, I noticed the door was ajar. *How convenient*, I thought, so I took a quick peak around the door.

The table was empty except for half of a jelly doughnut in a big open box, and one yellow coffee mug. No one was there, but I did hear a shuffling noise coming from beneath the table. I quickly ducked into the room, squatted down, and lifted up the flowered plastic tablecloth.

Harry looked like a turtle under the table, inspecting every inch of the wooden floor with his magnifying glass.

"Harry!" I whispered. "You're not supposed to be in here."

Harry looked up. "Oh, it's you, Doug! Hey, I finally have an important case. A missing diamond! It sounds like something Sherlock Holmes would investigate. I have to find that diamond for Miss Mackle. This is the last place she remembered seeing it."

"Okay, but we can't search now. We'll get in trouble. If you wait until after school, I'll go with you. My mom will be in the cafeteria with my brother's Cub Scout troop, so I need to stay late, anyway. We could explore then."

Harry crawled out from under the table. "It's a deal," he said, and we hurried to the door.

Unfortunately, Mr. Cardini, the principal, was just coming in. "What are you two doing here?" he asked.

We're doomed! I thought.

And that's when Harry reached for the coffee cup on the table. It had a big happy face on it. "Miss Mackle's mug," he answered. Now I recognized it. The teacher drank from it sometimes in class.

Mr. Cardini nodded. "Okay, boys," he said. "Have fun at the talent show on Friday! I hope to stop by and catch a few of the acts."

Talent show? I'd call it the torture show. I did *not* want to think about Friday!

The principal went over to the table and checked out the leftover jelly doughnut while Harry and I scooted down

the hallway with Miss Mackle's mug.

"You just told a fat fib!" I whispered.

"No, I didn't!" Harry insisted. "This *is* Miss Mackle's mug. I got it from the rack on the wall. I had it ready for an alibi, in case someone walked into the room. I didn't say she wanted it. I said it belonged to her."

Then Harry smiled like a jack-o'-lantern.

Harry! I thought.

When we got back to class, everyone

was still reading silently. Harry slid the cup behind the June Box on the teacher's desk and returned to his seat.

The only person who said anything was Mary. "What took you guys so long?" she whispered.

"Do you *really* want to know the smelly bathroom details?" Harry said, plopping into his chair.

Mary cringed, then went back to reading her hairdo book.

I looked up at our classroom clock and calculated the time. In one hundred and sixteen minutes Harry and I could snoop *after* school!

Chocolate Clues

At three thirty, Harry and I went to the cafeteria. School was out, so the only other kids in the building were six Tiger Pack Cub Scouts. My mom was passing out pretzels and pouring juice when we showed up. Supplies for building birdhouses sat on the table. My brother, Baxter, was punching the big sack of birdseed like it was a boxing bag. Even though he was just a first grader, Baxter hit like a heavyweight champion. I knew all about his punches.

"Mom!" I said. "Guess what?"

"I know," Mom groaned. "Baxter's teacher told me what happened. Poor Miss Mackle."

"Can we go help her look for the diamond?" I asked.

"What a good idea. Just come back here when Miss Mackle goes home."

"Okay!"

Then Mom added, "Doug, I was thinking that you could demonstrate

how to make a birdhouse for your talent show tomorrow. What do you think?"

I'd rather go to New Zealand. That's what I thought.

"Maybe," I said.

And we left.

When Harry and I got to Room 3B, our teacher was rooting around in her purse. "Hi, boys," she said.

"Doug's mom has Cub Scouts in the cafeteria," Harry explained. "She said we could help you look for your missing diamond, if you want."

"Oh, how nice." She stood up. "I have to make a call, but I'll be back . . . in a few minutes." Her voice got sad, and her eyes got watery.

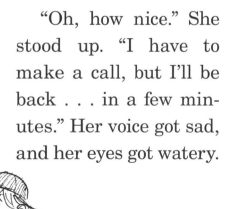

Then she left with her cell phone in her hand.

Harry and I immediately started our diamond search. I combed the white-board tray while he checked out the cracks in the wooden floor around the teacher's desk.

"Whoa, look at this, Dougo!" Harry cried out.

I dashed over with my journal. I wanted to record the exciting details.

Harry opened the bottom right drawer in the teacher's desk! Inside was a stash of . . . CHOCOLATE. There must have been three dozen pieces of foil-wrapped candy in the back, *and* a big pile of empty chocolate wrappers in front.

"*Harry!* What are you doing snooping in the teacher's drawers?"

"A good detective has to be thorough. This chocolate mine could be a clue! Now we know why Miss Mackle goes to her desk the first ten minutes of silent reading: she's craving a piece of chocolate."

"You'd better close that drawer right now!" I ordered.

Harry kept staring at the treasure chest of chocolate squares. "And this was one of the last places she was just before Song Lee screamed . . ."

Suddenly, we heard footsteps coming down the hall. Harry slammed the drawer shut and flopped onto the floor.

"Any luck, boys?" the teacher asked as she entered the room.

"Not yet," Harry answered.

Miss Mackle sank down into the beanbag chair just as Mr. Beausoleil

poked his head in the doorway. "I got your note, and I'm so sorry. I'll keep an eye out for that diamond, and put off cleaning the first floor. That way you'll have more time to look for it."

"Oh, thank you." Miss Mackle sighed. "Boys, do you want to come with me to the Teachers' Room now?"

"Sure!" we both said. I couldn't wait to search that place *with* permission.

Double Gross

Miss Mackle glanced at her desktop. "Oops, I forgot to return my coffee mug," she said.

I rolled my eyes at Harry. *He* was the one who put that mug there.

As soon as we got to the Teachers' Room, Harry checked out the table. There was a new package of Girl Scout cookies next to the empty doughnut box.

"Did you have a doughnut this morning?" Harry asked.

"Yes," Miss Mackle said.

"What flavor?"

"Chocolate frosted. Want a Thin Mint Cookie, boys?" she asked.

"Yes, please," I said.

Harry said no. He was too busy being a detective.

"Chocolate is my weakness," the teacher said. She took two cookies.

"No kidding?" Harry replied.

What a phony! Harry knew very well about the teacher's chocolate cravings. He was the one who discovered her chocolate drawer!

I took out my journal and continued listing places that we searched. Harry used his magnifying glass on the tiny chocolate smear on the side of the doughnut box. Miss Mackle lifted the pillows on the teachers' couch and looked underneath. I searched the sink drain. Harry got into his turtle stance and examined the rest of the floor.

Fifteen minutes later, Harry stood up. "No diamond," he groaned.

"I'm thinking it's not in this room," the teacher replied as she washed her hands at the sink.

Harry observed how she dried her hands with a brown paper towel, took a step back, and tossed it into the garbage can like a free throw. "Do you always wad up paper towels into tight balls like that?" he asked.

Miss Mackle chuckled. "I guess I do. I used to play basketball. It's easier to make the basket if it's wadded up like that."

"Your diamond could be tucked inside!" Harry said.

"Oh my goodness!" the teacher exclaimed.

Harry grabbed a newspaper from the table and spread it out on the floor. He dumped out the garbage can and fished around for paper towels. There were just three in tight wads. "These must be yours," he said.

Miss Mackle leaned forward as Harry tossed aside the first ball of paper. "You just used this one. It's still wet." He reached for the other two, then unraveled one.

"Chocolate frosting," Harry declared. "This is yours, all right."

Harry's investigation was beginning to gross me out.

He used his magnifying glass over each fold of the paper towel. "Not here."

Harry reached for the second paper ball. When he unfolded it, we could see two slimy orange things. Harry smelled them. "Peaches."

Double gross, I thought. Horrible stuff never bothered Harry. That was one talent I was glad I didn't have.

Miss Mackle made a face. "Peach yogurt, actually."

"No diamond," Harry said. Then he put everything back and washed his hands at the sink.

"Thanks, Harry." Miss Mackle sighed. "You're a hardworking detective."

Then her voice started to break up. "Thank you, too, Doug. I'm . . . going home now." I wondered if she was going to cry in her car.

"I'm not giving up!" Harry called out as we walked downstairs to the cafeteria.

Mom was helping kids scoop seeds into their milk carton birdhouses while my brother was punching her rear end. "Stop that, Baxter!" she scolded. Then she smiled at us. "Want to make a birdhouse, boys?" she asked. "There's still time."

I decided to give it a try. Maybe making one of those things for the talent show wasn't the *worst* idea in the world.

Harry was suddenly distracted. "Oh, man, I left my baseball cap in my desk. Be back in a jiff."

I nodded. I was busy gathering Popsicle sticks and twigs for my birdhouse.

Ten minutes later Harry came back . . . *without* his hat.

I was sitting at the end of the table, far away from my brother and his friends. They were having sword fights with the leftover Popsicle sticks.

"That diamond's not in the teachers' bathroom either," Harry whispered to me. "I checked it out."

"You went into the *teachers' bathroom*?" I repeated.

"I did. I couldn't snoop anymore in
Room 3B. Miss Mackle locked it on her
way out. But the Teachers' Room was
still open, and that's where the teachers'
bathroom is. There was a huge supply
of toilet paper in there. I counted fifty
rolls stacked up against the wall. That
should get them through June. Kind of
cool, actually. A TP tower!"

If anyone could find that diamond, it
would be Harry. He noticed *everything*!

Recess Rehearsals

The next morning, I felt like I had walked into a meat locker. "Look what that says, Harry!" I pointed to the whiteboard in our classroom.

Harry read the message that made my bones freeze up.

THIRD GRADE TALENT
SHOW—TOMORROW!
IN OUR ROOM AT 1:00 P.M.
BE PREPARED!

"So?" he said. "That's old news."

I pulled Harry aside. "You mean *chilling* news!" I replied. "I have the most boring act for tomorrow—how to make a birdhouse out of a milk carton."

"That's not boring," Harry said. "Birdhouses are cool."

"You don't think people will laugh at me?"

"No," Harry insisted. "You'll be great."

"Maybe." I groaned. "I just wish I had an exciting talent like you do—being a detective!"

"Well, my act is going to be a dud if I don't find the diamond."

Harry and I exchanged a look. It helped to share the misery.

At lunch recess, some of the girls and

Sidney rehearsed their talent show acts by the Dumpster. I could see and hear them when I was playing leftfield in kickball.

Ida was leaping on her toes. "I'm going to do a ballet dance!" she squealed. "Mom said I could even wear the costume from my last dance recital. It's a tutu."

"Too too what?" Sidney asked.

The girls giggled. "Sid," Ida explained, "a tutu is a little skirt that sticks out. Ballerinas wear them."

"Ohhh," Sid said.

"What are you doing, Mary?" Song Lee asked.

"Well, you know I have lots of talents.

It was hard to choose. But I decided to go with cooking. I'm going to demonstrate how to make strawberry parfaits with yogurt."

Song Lee clapped her hands. "I love strawberries!"

"What are you doing, Song Lee?" Ida asked.

Song Lee's happy face suddenly turned sad. "I made something in origami, but I may not be here tomorrow."

"Oh, I hope you will," Ida said. "I want to see what you made!"

"Me too," Mary added.

I understood Song Lee's feelings. She was too shy to do an act by herself in front of *both* third grades. She had only gone in front of our class twice before.

Once was when she stood behind a cherry tree and gave a short talk about Korea. The other time was when she was a dead fish in our Thanksgiving play.

Song Lee and I both needed to go to New Zealand.

Almost Showtime

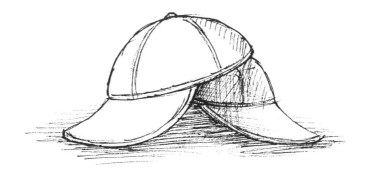

Friday morning everyone arrived with props for the third grade talent show. Dexter looked just like Elvis in his dark glasses, a gold necklace, and a white shirt. He had a guitar strapped to his shoulder.

"Look! Dexter is the king of rock and roll!" Mary gushed. "His cool hairstyle is called a pompadour in *The Guidebook of Fabulous Hairdos.*"

ZuZu was holding his clarinet case. "I can play 'Row, Row, Row Your Boat' by heart," he said.

Sid had a clown costume in a bag. He showed us his carrot-orange wig and ruffly collar. "I can juggle fruit!" he bragged.

Ida pulled her pink tutu out of a box and showed the girls. "I can't wait to do my pirouettes!" she exclaimed. Then she danced around on her toes.

I had no idea what *pirouettes* meant.

"What are you doing?" Sid asked me as we hung up our jackets in the coat closet.

I showed Sid my lopsided birdfeeder.

"I like el tweetos!" Sid said. "Lots of them are out now. It's spring. So where's the birdseed?" he asked.

Just as I lifted it up to show him, three Popsicle sticks fell off the roof. The twig I had used for a perch came untaped, and a bunch of birdseed spilled out onto the floor.

"Oh, no! I can't use this now. It's ruined!"

I cleaned up the mess and trudged to my desk.

Song Lee sat down next to me, holding a bag. She wasn't a happy camper either.

"What did you make?" I asked. I was surprised she even showed up at school today.

"An origami box." When she took it out and showed me, her hands shook.

It was the most beautiful paper box I had ever seen. It even had a paper rose on top of the lid.

"Wow! I wish I had your talent," I said. "You folded that whole thing?"

"Yes, but I'm not feeling too well."

Oh man, I thought. There was no way Song Lee was going to go on stage by herself.

Harry rushed to his desk. He had two baseball caps on. One brim was in front, the other was in the back. I knew why he wore them that way: he thought it looked like Sherlock Holmes's detective hat. His magnifying glass necklace was around his neck, outside his T-shirt.

"I see you're ready for your detective act," I said.

"Except for one small detail," he replied. "I have to find that diamond first."

I glanced at the clock. "You still have four hours. Hang in there, Harry."

"Thanks," he replied. Then he took a

long, hard look at Song Lee's box. "You made that?" Harry gasped.

"Yes," she answered.

"Your act is going to be the prettiest one in the show," he said. Song Lee stopped frowning when Harry flashed a toothy smile at her.

"So," Harry said turning to me. "Where's your birdhouse, Dougo?"

"In the garbage can. It's ruined. I'm hoping there's still time for me to pull something out of a hat."

"That's a bummer," Harry replied. "But I know you'll think of something good." Then he looked over at the teacher's desk. "There's still time for my secret raid, too."

Secret raid? During class? What was Harry up to this time?

Harry's Secret Raid

Shortly after eleven o'clock, I found out what Harry's secret raid was. We were all working on morning math at our desks, except for Sidney and Dexter. They were sitting at the front round table with Miss Mackle. She was showing them how to add mixed fractions, using cardboard pizza slices.

Harry got up to sharpen his pencil, but he took the long way around Miss

Mackle's desk. I watched him drop his pencil on purpose, duck down, and stick his hand in the bottom drawer. He fished out a huge handful of chocolates and stuffed them in his jeans pocket! Then he sharpened his pencil and returned to his desk.

His secret raid was on the teacher's chocolate drawer!

As soon as he sat down, I whispered, "Harry! What are you doing?"

Harry put a finger up to his mouth. Then he stood up and did the same thing *again*!

And then a *third* time!

"Done!" he said plopping in his chair. His jeans pockets were bulging with chocolate squares.

"Harry Spooger!" I whispered. "I can't believe you're stealing Miss Mackle's chocolate!"

Harry reared back. He looked insulted. "I'm no thief!" he insisted. "And I didn't take any of her chocolates. I just took the empty wrappers."

I was relieved, but very confused. "The empty chocolate wrappers? Why?"

Harry lowered his head and whispered, "The diamond could have fallen inside her chocolate drawer when she reached for a piece of candy. It might be inside one of the empty wrappers in the front. I'm checking these sweet babies at recess." Then he patted both pockets.

I slid down in my chair and thought about it. I guessed it could work.

Harry took his fingers and zipped his lip.

I did the same thing. His secret raid was safe with me.

As soon as I finished my math, I took out my writing journal to brainstorm ideas. What could I do for the talent show? Nothing dumb. It would be embarrassing if anyone laughed at me.

Wait a minute. That was an idea! Maybe I should *try* to make people laugh.

After lunch, we went outside to recess. Harry sat by the Dumpster, going through each of those chocolate wrappers. I didn't play kickball either. I leaned against the fence, writing down

knock-knock jokes. So far I had one:

Knock knock.
Who's there?
Radio.
Radio who?
Radio not, here I come.

Then I remembered a joke Harry

told me in second grade, and I wrote
that down too:

Did you hear about the two
cannon balls that got married?
They had a little BB.

When the recess bell rang, and it
was time to go inside, Harry went to the
end of the line and pulled his Sherlock
Holmes hat down over his eyes. I knew
exactly how he felt. I didn't have anything for the talent show, either. My
knock-knock joke was stupid, and everyone has heard the cannonball joke. That
was really a bomb.

Miss Mackle's diamond wasn't the
only thing missing. So was my talent!

The Nose Knows

As we walked back to the classroom, I noticed that Harry ducked into the nurse's office. Was he sick? I followed him inside.

Song Lee was sitting in a chair. Two other kids sat on her left: a girl with a bloody scrape on her knee and a boy with an ice pack on his head. The nurse was on the phone.

Harry sat next to Song Lee. I plopped down next to Harry.

"What are you doing here, Song Lee?" Harry asked.

"I don't feel well. I have a stomachache."

"You can't go home," Harry said. "I need you to be my assistant!"

"For what?" she asked.

Harry looked at both of us. "Can you two keep a *very important* secret?"

We nodded, then moved our heads closer to Harry's.

"I found Miss Mackle's diamond in an empty chocolate raspberry square wrapper!"

Song Lee squealed, then covered her mouth. I rolled up my journal and bopped Harry on the head. When the nurse started to shush us, we got up and left.

"You really found it?" I gasped as we hurried down the hallway.

"Yes!" Harry replied. "I tried to hide my face when we lined up after recess because I wanted to save the good news for the talent show. But when I saw Song Lee, I remembered her origami box. I knew I needed a better container for the diamond."

"Where is the diamond now?" I asked.

When Harry stopped walking, we did too.

He pulled out an empty sandwich Baggie from his right pocket. It had a streak of peanut butter and jelly in one corner. It was a leftover bag from his lunch box. A horrible place for a diamond!

Harry handed it to Song Lee. "Here, take this. You're my assistant. Make sure the diamond is safely tucked away in your beautiful box."

Song Lee carefully held on to the Baggie with two hands. We could see the diamond at the bottom. It still sparkled through the plastic. Song Lee moved the bag close to her heart, then scooted back to our classroom. She was on an important mission now for Miss Mackle!

Harry grabbed my shirt and pulled

me aside. "Doug, that diamond was under the teacher's nose all this time. *In her desk!* That's what Grandma always tells me when I'm looking for something. She says, *It's probably right under your nose.*" Then he added, "Only, I would say, *right under your schnozzola.*"

And that's when I looked down and noticed what I was holding in my hand. "Holy moly!" I exclaimed. Harry had just told me where to find my talent!

The Talent Show

As soon as we got to the classroom, Miss Mackle greeted us. "Song Lee told me you were in the nurse's office with her. Hurry up boys, we're about ready to start our talent show!"

Our class sat down on the floor. The other third grade class came in and sat down on the desks that were pushed to the wall behind us. One by one, kids performed their talent show acts. ZuZu's clarinet solo was very short. Mary's cooking lesson was long.

Ida twirled and leaped gracefully on her toes to classical music.

Dexter sang Elvis's song "Hound Dog" while he danced around the room, strumming his guitar.

Sidney only dropped two oranges in his clown juggling act.

When it was my turn, I took my writing journal with me to the front of the room. I was excited that Mr. Cardini was standing in the doorway.

"I had a hard time thinking of my talent," I said. "And then I looked under my nose and saw my journal. I usually have it with me. My favorite thing to do is write. I've written twenty-nine stories so far. Most of them were inspired by things that happen in Room 3B. This

one is called 'Harold and the Quadruple Revenge.'"

Everyone was pin quiet while I read my story. *That's a good sign*, I thought. They even laughed at the funny parts.

". . . and so Martha never tattled on Harold again. They shook hands and remained friends."

"I love happy endings!" Mary blurted out.

The audience clapped, and Miss

Mackle waved her arms in the air. Mr. Cardini called out, "Bravissimo!"

I felt so good, I gave my journal a kiss!

Two hours later, we were down to the finale: Harry and Song Lee's act.

Harry walked up to the stage area with a large garbage bag. He pushed two desks together in front of him, then motioned for Song Lee to come up. She did, but she stood a little behind Harry.

"As you know," he said, "our teacher, Miss Mackle, lost one diamond from her engagement ring. We all have been looking for it. Especially me. I'm a detective." He took a moment to adjust his Sherlock Holmes hat before he continued. "A detective usually has an assistant. I have a great one: Song Lee Park." When everyone clapped, Song

Lee looked down at her shoes. I don't think she wanted to see forty-five faces staring at her.

"A detective looks for clues," Harry continued. "Sometimes they're good ones, and sometimes they're duds. They don't lead you anywhere. I'm going to show you four possible clues in the Case of the Missing Diamond."

Harry started pulling out items from his bag.

"Round pieces of masking tape from the trash can, exhibit A," he said, sticking a few onto the desktop.

Lots of kids leaned forward for a better look.

"A doughnut box from the Teachers' Room, exhibit B."

"Two wadded-up brown paper towels, exhibit C."

All the while, Song Lee kept her
hands behind her back.

"And . . ." Harry held up a finger.
"This is exhibit D." He dropped a handful of empty chocolate wrappers on the
desktop.

Miss Mackle raised her eyebrows.

I was glad Harry didn't tell *where* he found the wrappers. No one needed to know that Miss Mackle had a secret drawer in her desk just for chocolate!

Then Harry made a gesture toward Song Lee. "Ta-dah!"

Very slowly, Song Lee brought her hands around to the front and showed what she was holding

It was her origami box.

Everyone oohed and ahhed!

"Miss Mackle," Harry said. "Would you please come here and open this up."

Everyone leaned forward.

"I can't wait to see what's inside!" Sidney blurted out.

The Inside Story

Everyone watched Miss Mackle lift the paper lid off Song Lee's origami box.

Suddenly the teacher's eyes bulged.

"My diamond!" she exclaimed.

Everyone burst into cheers.

"Where in the world did you find it, Harry?" Miss Mackle asked.

"In a sweet place," he said, holding up an empty chocolate square wrapper.

"Exhibit D!" a few kids called out.

Everyone stood up and clapped.

Mary pushed her way to the front. "But exactly where did you find that chocolate wrapper?" she demanded.

Harry started putting the items back into his garbage bag. "Mare, a good detective *never* reveals his sources. He has to protect people's privacy." Then he grinned at the teacher.

Miss Mackle's face turned pink. Now she knew that Harry knew about her secret drawer!

Ida and Mary rushed over to Song Lee. The three girls made a huddle and bounced up and down.

Miss Mackle got happy tears in her eyes. *"Thank you,* Harry! You should open up your own detective agency. May I keep this beautiful box for a little while?"

Song Lee called out, "It's yours, Miss Mackle!"

As soon as the other third grade class left Room 3B, Miss Mackle went back to her desk. "Harry, can I see you for a moment?" she said.

Harry slung the garbage bag onto his back then zipped over to see her.

They exchanged a few words, and Miss Mackle gave Harry a hug.

I followed Harry to the garbage can. He dumped the black bag inside, then jumped on top of it. "Great job, Sherlock!" I said.

Harry made two V for victory signs with his fingers. "It was my best case ever! I think your quadruple revenge story was your best, too."

"Well, thanks for helping me find my talent." I held up my journal.

Harry suddenly stopped jumping and looked down at his shirt. "My great-grandpa's necklace! It's not there. I think I just stomped it to smithereens."

Harry immediately leaped out and started rooting for it in the garbage can.

"Maybe you're still wearing it?" I suggested.

Harry reached inside his T-shirt and pulled out the magnifying glass, still in one piece. "Phew, it was there all along. Right under my . . ."

"Schnozzola!" we both said. After we laughed, I had to ask, "So what did Miss Mackle say to you?"

"She thanked me and gave me a reward. I promised her I wouldn't go into her desk again."

"What was the reward?" I whispered.

"I'm sharing it with you, Dougo." Harry handed me one of his two foil-wrapped chocolate squares.

"Ahhh . . . we finally get to taste one," I whispered.

"At last!" Harry said, flashing a toothy smile.